Silly Milly

For my grandson Joshua—
who likes silly stories, but does not like sad ones.
—Wendy Lewison

For Elise,
Love Deanie.

Text copyright © 2010 by Wendy Lewison
Illustrations copyright © 2010 by Nadine Bernard Westcott, Inc.

All rights reserved. Published by Scholastic Inc.
SCHOLASTIC, CARTWHEEL BOOKS, and associated logos
are trademarks and/or registered trademarks of Scholastic Inc.
Lexile is a registered trademark of MetaMetrics, Inc.

Library of Congress Cataloging-in-Publication Data

Lewison, Wendy Cheyette.
Silly Milly / by Wendy Lewison ; illustrated by Nadine Bernard Westcott.
p. cm.
"Cartwheel books."
Summary: Invites the reader to solve the riddle of why Silly Milly likes certain
things and dislikes others.
ISBN-13: 978-0-545-06859-8
ISBN-10: 0-545-06859-2
[1. Stories in rhyme. 2. Likes and dislikes--Fiction. 3. Riddles--Fiction.] I.
Westcott, Nadine Bernard, ill. II. Title.

PZ8.3.L592Sil 2010
[E]--dc22

2008022456

ISBN: 978-0-545-06859-8
32 31 30 29   18 19/0
Printed in the U.S.A. 40 • First printing, April 2010

Silly Milly

By Wendy Cheyette Lewison
Illustrated by Nadine Bernard Westcott

SCHOLASTIC INC.

This is a riddle
about Miss Milly.
Can you guess why
she is so silly?

She likes green.
She does not like red.

She likes butter.
She does not like bread.

She likes seeds.

She does not like flowers.

She likes umbrellas.
She does not like showers.

She likes alligators.

She does not like mice.

She likes snowballs.
She does not like ice.

She likes needles.
She does not like to sew.

She likes grass.
She does not like to mow.

She likes green peppers.

She does not like pickles.

She likes pennies.

She does not like nickels.

She likes cabbage.
She does not like pie.

Miss Milly is so silly!
Can you tell why?